Mommy Ant, Eat Your Vegetables!

Written by **Sigmund Brouwer**

Illustrated by **Sharon Dahl**

Created by **Don Sullivan**

Tommy
NELSON®

Thomas Nelson, Inc.
Nashville

Published in Nashville, Tennessee, by Tommy Nelson®,
a division of Thomas Nelson, Inc.

Scripture quotations used in this book are from the Holy Bible,
New Century Version, copyright © 1987, 1988, 1991 by Word Publishing,
Nashville, Tennessee. Used by permission.

Library of Congress Cataloging-in-Publication Data

Brouwer, Sigmund, 1959-
  Mommy Ant, eat your vegetables / written by Sigmund Brouwer ;
illustrated by Sharon Dahl ; created by Don Sullivan
    p. cm.—(Bug's-eye view books)
  Summary: Mommy Ant and her family realize the importance of
eating their vegetables.
  ISBN 0-8499-7733-9
  [1. Food habits—Fiction. 2. Nutrition—Fiction. 3. Ants—Fiction.]
I. Dahl, Sharon, ill. II. Sullivan, Don, 1953- III. Title. IV. Series.

PZ7.B79984 Mm 2001
[E]—dc21   2001034516

Printed in Italy
01 02 03 04 05 PBI 5 4 3 2 1

THe BibLe SaYs . . .

And those who eat
all kinds of food are doing
that for the Lord, and they
give thanks to God.

–Romans 14:6b

"Remember everyone,"
Mommy Ant said, "eat
your vegetables, and
you will grow up
healthy and
strong."

"Can you believe it?" Arnie Ant
suddenly shouted. "Can it be?"

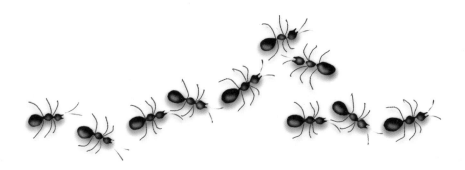

"Keep looking!" cried Annie Ant.

"I'm sure I saw something!"

"It must be gone," Arnie Ant said.

"Hush, Baby Ant," said Annie Ant
when her sister began to whine.
"Have something to eat."

"Annie Ant, I'm glad you
ate your vegetables,"
Mommy Ant said. "If
you didn't, you would
grow up to have bad
eyes and bad teeth.
Would you like that
on your wedding day?"

"Arnie Ant," said Mommy Ant,
"I'm glad you ate your
vegetables. If you didn't,
you would grow up to have
bad bones and weak muscles.
Would you like that in college?"

"Arnie Ant, why didn't you eat your vegetables?" asked Mommy Ant.
"Annie Ant, why didn't you eat your vegetables?"

"Mommy Ant," said Arnie Ant,
"you never eat your vegetables."

"Mommy Ant," said Annie Ant,
"we want to be like you."

"If you don't eat your vegetables,"
asked Annie Ant, "will you have
bad eyes and bad teeth
when you grow old?"

"If you don't eat your vegetables,"
asked Arnie Ant, "will you have
bad bones and weak muscles
when you grow old?"